Fish Had a Wish

Fish Had a Wish

Michael Garland

SCHOLASTIC INC.

ISBN 978-0-545-49989-7

Copyright © 2012 by Michael Garland.
All rights reserved. Published by Scholastic Inc.,
557 Broadway, New York, NY 10012,
by arrangement with Holiday House, Inc.
I LIKE TO READ is a registered trademark of Holiday House, Inc.
SCHOLASTIC and associated logos are trademarks
and/or registered trademarks of Scholastic Inc.

12 11 10 9 8 7 6 5 4 3 2 1   13 14 15 16 17 18/0

Printed in the U.S.A.   40

First Scholastic printing, January 2013

The text typeface is Report School.
The artwork was created in digi-wood.

To my mother

Fish had a wish.

"I wish I were a bird!"
said Fish.
"I could fly high up
in the sky."

"I wish I were a turtle.
I could take a nap
on a sunny rock."

"I wish I were a skunk.
I could make a big stink!"

"If I were a bobcat,
I could have spots."

"If I were a bee,
I could buzz
from flower to flower."

"I could be a beaver
and build a big dam."

"I could be a butterfly with pretty wings."

"I wish I were a snake.
HISSSSSSS."

A mayfly landed on the water.
Fish ate the bug with one bite.
"That was *so good!*"
said Fish.

"It is good to be a fish.
I wish to *stay* a fish.
Yes!
To stay a fish is
what I wish."